THE WORLD OF JOJO

THE WORLD OF JOJO

VIPASHA SHARMA

First Printing, 2025

To all the hearts that believe in kindness—
that know there is a soul in every living being,
and a story in every love.

This tale is for the children
who speak with the forests,
and for the elders
who still believe in childhood.

Acknowledgments

In every word of this story, there is a debt owed—to those who taught me that love is not limited to humans.

I am grateful to my family, friends, and all the readers who gave me the confidence that the language of emotions can be understood by every heart, be it human or animal.

Special thanks to all the souls that dwell in the forest, the river, and every corner of life—because they are the true inspiration for this story.

— Vipasha Sharma

The Shepherd, the Fish, and the Gift of a Son

A shepherd and his wife lived in a forest. They had a small, mud-house, and their life was very simple and happy.

Every morning, the shepherd would take his goats and sheep into the dense forest, and his wife would also go with him. Together, they would let the animals graze on the green grass and relax by the riverbank.

They had no children, which often filled the shepherd's wife with sadness. She frequently wished that they could have a child to bring a new turn to their lives.

One day, while grazing their animals, they reached the riverbank. The river water was clean and sparkling, with gentle ripples playing on the surface. Suddenly, the shepherd's wife noticed something in the river: a large fish was thrashing about, caught in a net.

The shepherd's wife grew anxious and said, "Look, this fish is trapped in a net. It will die if it isn't freed."

Saying this, the shepherd's wife gathered her courage and waded into the water. She opened the net and released the fish back into the river. As soon as the fish swam free, the river suddenly glowed with a golden light.

Then, a voice spoke, and the fish transformed into a beautiful woman, who smiled and said, "I was given the form of a fish due to a curse, and that curse could only be broken if someone helped me."

"You both showed kindness. You helped me by freeing me from this net and gave me a new life. I grant you a boon: you will soon be blessed with a son."

After saying this, the woman disappeared.

The shepherd and his wife looked at each other with joy and returned home.

Time passed, and the day came when the shepherd's wife gave birth to a beautiful son. The sounds of a child's laughter echoed in their home. The baby's cries made it seem as if spring had arrived in the forest ahead of season. The entire forest rejoiced, peacocks began to dance, and cuckoos sang sweet songs. Flower buds blossomed. All the animals came to the shepherd's house to see the child.

The child was extremely beautiful; his eyes were deep and bright like a fish's, as if the river's sparkle resided within them. His feet were as soft and lovely as lotus petals. His skin was as cool as moonlight.

The shepherd and his wife were filled with immense joy upon seeing their son.

The shepherd and his wife named the child Jojo.

Jojo's Adventure and the Forest Friend

Slowly, time passed.

Little Jojo began to grow up. As Jojo grew, so did his mischief. Sometimes he would roll around in the mud in the courtyard, sometimes he would grab the goats' tails and run, and sometimes he would play by filling his mother's utensils with water. His laughter filled the whole house with light.

However, Jojo had one constant demand: he wanted to go with his father into the dense forest to herd the goats. Jojo was still very small, so his mother would laugh and scold him every time. Jojo would be filled with sadness and start to cry.

One day, while playing, he wandered off alone toward the dense forest.

Jojo started to feel scared seeing the thick forest. Tall trees blocked even the sunlight. Birds were chirping, and the air was cool. But as the sun began to set, the forest's color changed. The shadows of the trees grew long, the birds fell silent, and a strange stillness spread everywhere.

Jojo looked around and began to cry. He waited for his father, then ran and sat down under a large tree, weeping.

Suddenly, a sound came from the bushes. Jojo was terrified. He bravely got up, wiped his tears, and saw a small puppy coming towards him!

The puppy wagged its tail, came close to him, and started licking his hands. Jojo was delighted to see him and started to laugh. Jojo began to play with him and picked him up to pet him. They both found comfort in each other, and their fear disappeared.

A little later, Jojo's father found them. He had been looking for Jojo and reached the same spot where Jojo was sleeping under the tree with his new friend. As Jojo opened his eyes, he saw his father and started to cry, hugging him tightly. Jojo and his father started to head home, and the puppy followed them.

The next morning, Jojo told his mother that he wanted to keep his new friend, and she gave a gentle smile.

Now, Jojo started living with the puppy. Jojo named the puppy Tommy.

Time went by.

Jojo and Tommy also grew older. Now they went everywhere together—sometimes playing, sometimes sitting by the river, and sometimes running in the forest. Their friendship deepened.

Jojo and Tommy would play together, eat together, and bathe near the pond.

Jojo's Lesson and the Fisherman's Curse

Jojo and Tommy were always together.

Jojo was now grown up. He started going with his father to the dense forest to graze the goats. Whenever the goats ran off, Tommy would immediately bark and round them up into one place. This is how he helped Jojo. Jojo's father was very happy to see his son and Tommy working together. Jojo and Tommy went to the dense forest every day to work and play. In the evening, they would bring the sheep and goats home with Jojo's father.

One day during the summer, they went to the river for a swim, as they often did. They wandered until they reached the same spot where Jojo's parents had received the boon. Jojo and Tommy both jumped into the water and began swimming merrily. They chased each other and laughed. Their laughter echoed throughout the forest.

Suddenly, Jojo noticed a small baby fish swimming in the water. Jojo caught the fish and started playing with it. But in the midst of his play, he took the fish out of the water, and in a short while, the fish died. Tommy saw the dead fish and started to eat it.

Just then, a large fish emerged from the river. Tears were in her eyes, and she said, "Just as you took my child's life, your Tommy will also die, and you will be left alone like me." After saying this, the fish swam deep into the water.

Jojo started to tremble with fear. The fish slipped from his hand. Jojo began to cry loudly and looked at Tommy with sad eyes. Jojo hugged Tommy tightly. Seeing the tears flowing from Jojo's eyes, Tommy's eyes also became moist.

With a heavy heart, Jojo returned home. Crying, he told his parents everything that had happened. His mother held him close and said, "In life, we should never harm any creature, and we must protect all living beings."

His parents' eyes also welled up with tears upon seeing Jojo.

From that day on, Jojo resolved that he would never trouble any living creature again and would protect them. However, Jojo remained sad. The fear that Tommy might leave him was always visible in his eyes.

The Sacrifice of Friendship

A long time passed, and slowly, Jojo began to forget his grief and the curse. He started playing with Tommy again. They spent their days wandering in the forests, running along the riverbanks. Now, even the wild animals of the forest had become their friends. Deer, rabbits, peacocks, and even some wild monkeys would come closer as soon as they saw them.

However, one day, a group of hunters suddenly arrived in the forest. They began mercilessly hunting the animals. Seeing this, Jojo's heart felt heavy. Tears welled up in his innocent eyes. That night, he made a silent resolve: that he would never back down from saving his friends and the wild animals.

The next morning, Jojo and Tommy began building a strong wooden fence all around the forest. This was not an easy task; the forest was vast, but Jojo did not lose hope. Slowly, he created a safe area where the animals could live fearlessly.

Time continued to move forward, and shortly after, Jojo's mother fell ill and passed away because they couldn't get treatment. Broken-hearted by the loss of his wife, Jojo's father also bid farewell to the world a few days later.

Now, Jojo and Tommy were alone. They had to be each other's support.Time continued to move forward, and shortly after, Jojo's mother fell ill and passed away because they couldn't get treatment. Broken-hearted by the loss of his wife, Jojo's father also bid farewell to the world a few days later.

Now, Jojo and Tommy were alone. They had to be each other's support.

After some time, Tommy also started being quiet and withdrawn. It was as if he sensed that his end was near. Tommy began to distance himself from Jojo.

One night, Jojo was fast asleep when he had a terrible dream. He remembered the curse and saw the fish again. Jojo woke up scared. A wave of fear and sadness ran through his heart. As soon as morning came, he ran to the same riverbank where he had once caught the baby fish. He began to cry loudly.

Suddenly, the river water started to shine. A golden light rose from it, and the same fish, who was now in the form of a woman, appeared. Her voice was deep and melodious. She told Jojo the way to break the curse:

"Jojo, there is only one way to break the curse. You must sacrifice Tommy. If you keep him with you, the curse will kill him. But if you separate yourself from him, he will live."

Hearing this, Jojo's heart broke. The thought of living without Tommy was impossible for him. But he knew there was no other way to save his friend's life.

For a few days, he stopped talking to Tommy. He neither played with him nor called him close. Tommy would look at him sadly.

Finally, one day, Jojo took Tommy out of the forest and left him on the road that led to the city. Tears streamed non-stop from his eyes. Tommy looked at Jojo, and Jojo told Tommy to go away. Saying this, Jojo ran back towards the forest. Tommy wanted to chase after him, but Jojo quickly returned into the forest.

Slowly, time passed, and the curse was broken. Tommy remained alive, but now they were separated.

Tommy returned to the forest every day to search for Jojo. He would sense Jojo's scent but would always return to the city disappointed. Meanwhile, Jojo established himself in a different part of the forest. Working alone, he built a large house, where his goats, sheep, and the forest animals became his companions.

Jojo always remembered Tommy and wept.

Jojo, the Healer, and the New Journey

Jojo worked hard day and night, spending his time grazing sheep and goats. Jojo now also prepared medicines from herbs and helped the animals. Slowly, Jojo developed a good understanding of herbs.

During those days, a disease was spreading in the city. Some city folk would go to the forest to gather wood. Jojo had become well-acquainted with these people. The people told Jojo about the illness spreading in the city and asked him to go to the city to find a cure.

Listening to them, Jojo decided to head towards the city. He brought his sheep and goats home before evening. Jojo set off towards the city with the people.

Jojo visited people's houses, observed the illness, and told them that he would soon bring the cure. The next day, Jojo headed towards the dense forest, past the Black Cave and towards the mountains.

After some time, Jojo gathered all the herbs and started heading back home. On the way, when he reached the Black

Cave, he saw many mongooses coming out. Their paws and teeth were stained with blood. Jojo quickly went inside the Black Cave and saw a baby python lying there, covered in blood.

Jojo treated the baby python and moved it to another location where no one could harm it. It had become very late. As Jojo tried to exit the dense forest, he lost his way. Suddenly, a fierce storm began, and he found himself under the same tree where he had first met Tommy as a child.

Jojo sat down at that spot and started remembering his old days. Jojo remembered Tommy and began to cry. After some time, Jojo fell asleep there. When morning began, Jojo saw that the weather had cleared, and he could now return home. Jojo went home and began to prepare the medicine from those herbs.

A few days later, the medicine was ready, and Jojo set off towards the city. He went to the city and started treating the people, who slowly began to recover.

After a few days, the people's illness was completely cured. Everyone was talking about Jojo. Jojo was very happy to hear all this.

However, some people in the city disliked Jojo because he started being invited to every small and big festival and was shown great affection. Seeing all this, those people grew jealous of Jojo.

After some time, Jojo made friends with a girl. Everyone called this girl Julie. Julie was very beautiful.

Jojo, Julie, and the Rebirth of the Forest

Jojo and Julie became very good friends. Julie started going with Jojo to the forest to collect herbs. However, people did not approve of this. The people who disliked Jojo started spreading rumors about Jojo and Julie in the city. Julie's parents forbade her from leaving the house.

One day, Julie ran away from her home and went into the forest. People saw her and, taking flaming torches in their hands, set off toward the forest.

The people set the forest on fire to burn Jojo's house. As soon as Jojo stepped out of his house, he saw Julie running. Julie came to Jojo and told him everything. Then, Jojo saw that the fire was spreading rapidly throughout the entire forest. Jojo quickly released his sheep and goats and led them to a safe spot on the other side of the forest.

Jojo and Julie started returning towards their home and saw that it was completely engulfed in flames. Jojo cried, looking at the whole forest.

The next morning, when the fire was extinguished, Jojo and Julie gathered all the injured animals in the forest and brought them to a safe place. Jojo and Julie worked together to treat them.

Jojo and Julie began moving all the sheep and goats to another location.

After wandering for some time, Jojo went with Julie to his old home—the one where he had lived with his parents. Julie and Jojo began living there. Jojo would often go to the special tree, spend some time there, and remember Tommy.

One day, Julie went with Jojo to graze the sheep and goats. When Jojo started going towards the tree, Julie asked him why he sat in that specific spot. Jojo told Julie the entire story of his childhood, which made Julie cry.

Julie told Jojo that he should go to the city and look for Tommy. But Jojo refused to go toward the city.

Some years later...

Jojo and Julie were blessed with twins. Their son was handsome like Jojo and had bright, shining eyes like his. Their daughter was beautiful like Julie, with soft feet.

Jojo was very happy with his family.

The Reunion and Farewell

As time passed, the children grew a little older.

Jojo frequently had to go towards the city for household errands. One day, returning from the city, he stopped for a brief rest near the special tree in the middle of the forest. Suddenly, lightning began to flash, and dark clouds gathered in the sky. Jojo started to head home, but then he heard a voice coming from the river.

Jojo quickly ran towards the river and saw an animal had fallen in. Due to the darkness, Jojo couldn't see clearly. As he entered the river, he heard Tommy's voice. Jojo pulled the animal out of the water and realized it was none other than his Tommy.

Seeing Tommy in this condition filled Jojo with great sorrow, and he brought him home. Tommy was now old and couldn't run properly.

But after a few days, Tommy's wounds healed. Julie and the children were very happy to see Tommy. The children played with Tommy, sometimes pulling his ears, sometimes cleaning his teeth.

However, a few months later, Tommy passed away. He said his final goodbye to Jojo before he died.

Born in 2002 in Himachal Pradesh, Vipasha Sharma has always been fascinated by the way people think, feel, and respond to the world. Her stories reflect her belief that every individual, human or animal, carries a unique emotional universe. Drawing from her own experiences and observations, she writes with a focus on compassion, gentle wisdom, and the value of perspective. Through her books, she invites readers to slow down, reflect, and find meaning in everyday moments.

9 789334 455823

Printed at Repro India Ltd.